THE STA

T0040346

Humans are the most successful animals on the planet Earth – successful, that is, in the fight with other animals. If it's a question of fighting for food or land, then we humans always win. We cut down trees, build houses and factories, grow our own food. The animals must go and find another place to live . . . if they can.

We humans always win because we are intelligent. We can think, talk, use tools, make wonderful machines. We are extremely clever animals . . .

Perhaps too clever. Perhaps people in the future will think differently. Hummingbird (Hummy for short) is a girl of sixteen who lives in about 22,500 AD, on a planet a long way from Earth. She likes clothes and dancing, and worries about who she will marry. She has never seen a tree. She has never seen any animal or bird. She knows what animals are, of course, because there are stories about them in the Book of Remembering. But who can believe old stories like that?

OXFORD BOOKWORMS LIBRARY

Fantasy & Horror

The Star Zoo

Stage 3 (1000 headwords)

Series Editor: Jennifer Bassett
Founder Editor: Tricia Hedge
Activities Editors: Jennifer Bassett and Christine Lindop

For Will

HARRY GILBERT

The Star Zoo

OXFORD UNIVERSITY PRESS

OXFORD

UNIVERSITY PRESS

Great Clarendon Street, Oxford OX2 6DP

Oxford University Press is a department of the University of Oxford.
It furthers the University's objective of excellence in research, scholarship,
and education by publishing worldwide in

Oxford New York

Auckland Cape Town Dar es Salaam Hong Kong Karachi
Kuala Lumpur Madrid Melbourne Mexico City Nairobi
New Delhi Shanghai Taipei Toronto

With offices in

Argentina Austria Brazil Chile Czech Republic France Greece
Guatemala Hungary Italy Japan Poland Portugal Singapore
South Korea Switzerland Thailand Turkey Ukraine Vietnam

OXFORD and OXFORD ENGLISH are registered trade marks of
Oxford University Press in the UK and in certain other countries

ISBN 978 0 19 479131 1

Printed in China

Illustrated by: Craig Phillips/Shannon Associates

Word count (main text): 8915 words

For more information on the Oxford Bookworms Library,
visit www.oup.com/bookworms

CONTENTS

1
You must marry me

Nothing ever happens on Just Like Home – that's the name of the planet I live on. I get so bored!

But tonight was Remembering Night and that's exciting. There's the big fire where everybody must put on something that they love and watch it burn. Then there's the dancing round the fire.

But what I like best about Remembering Night are the clothes. We usually wear what we like on Just Like Home – but the clothes must have the name of our name-animal on them. For example, I always have the word 'Hummingbird' on my clothes, which means my name is Hummingbird – Hummy for short.

Nobody knows what a hummingbird looks like, but we know what birds are. Birds are animals that fly. The Book of Remembering tells us that.

I don't always believe what the Book of Remembering says.

Nobody knows who you are on Remembering Night because you wear black clothes that cover you from head to foot, and there is no name of your name-animal. You can only see people's eyes looking out of the eye-holes in the clothes.

It was dark outside. The only light came from the big fire. I held my father's hand at first and we danced together. My mother danced away and I couldn't see her. Soon I lost my father. I didn't know where they were.

It didn't matter. I was dancing in the middle of the crowd. Our family would meet together in the robot plane afterwards.

There were about a thousand people round the fire. Too many people to count. Nearly everybody on Just Like Home was there.

Everybody, on planets all over the Galaxy, was dancing round fires at the same time. What a wonderful thing!

The last dance began. You hold hands in a big circle round the fire – everybody together. You dance round and round in a circle until . . .

Well, everybody knows what happens in the end.

I was holding hands with someone on my right and someone on my left. We were all shouting, 'BURN BURN BURN BURN BURN BURN BURN . . .'

The last dance went on for a long time. In the end somebody fell down. He pulled down the people on both sides of him. Then people on both sides of *them* fell down. Everybody was too tired to stay on their feet.

People fell down all round the circle. Falling. Dying.

We wear black clothes to remember. We remember the Burning.

We remember that we have a Galaxy, but we are alone. We are empty in our hearts. We are the only living things in the Galaxy.

Sad. Lonely and sad.

I lay on the ground, very, very tired. I was happy and sad at the same time. Happy to be with everybody, sad that we

The last dance began. You hold hands in a big circle round the fire –
everybody together.

were alone.

Then the worst thing in my life happened. Somebody came up to me and said, 'Hello.' I didn't know who it was. I could only see his eyes shining in the light of the fire. But it was the voice of a man who was much older than me.

'Hello?' I answered. I didn't want to talk to him.

'I saw you in the dance,' he said. 'I know you're a young girl because you were dancing like a young girl. I think you're seventeen years old.'

'No, I'm only sixteen,' I said.

'Wonderful. Just what I want,' said the man. 'I will marry you. You must marry me.'

I couldn't believe what he was saying. This was terrible. And very bad luck.

Yes, it was true a woman must marry any man who asks her on Remembering Night – by order of the Star Council. I'm sixteen so I'm a woman, not a child. I couldn't say no to this man. I was sick in my heart.

'My name's Buff,' the man said. 'What's your name, sweetheart?'

'Er, my name's, er . . . Caterpillar,' I lied. 'I'm usually called Kate.'

'Well, Kate,' Buff said, 'will you marry me?'

'I'm sorry, Buff. I know I'm sixteen and old enough to get married but my parents don't want me to get married yet. I'm their only daughter.'

Buff laughed. It was a horrible laugh. He enjoyed knowing I didn't want him. What a monster!

Oh, thank Earth-and-animals I hadn't told him my real name!

I jumped up suddenly and ran into the crowds of people in the dark. I was safe. He couldn't find me. I went to our robot plane and sat inside until my parents came.

I didn't tell my parents anything. I was afraid. The Star Council said Buff was right and I was wrong, and I didn't know what my parents would do.

Next morning I forgot about it. How could Buff find me? There were hundreds of girls on our planet. He didn't know my name. He had only seen my eyes.

Suddenly my father came into my room. 'Hummingbird,' he said sadly.

'What's the matter?' I asked. 'Why are you calling me Hummingbird, not Hummy?'

'Hummingbird, ask your robot for a wedding dress.'

'Why? Why?' But I knew the answer.

'You will marry a gentleman called Buffalo.'

'No, father, I can't.' I started crying. 'I don't want to. I'm too young. I don't want to leave you. I hate him!'

My father shook his head. 'Please, Hummy, it's only for one year. You can't be a child forever. Lots of girls don't want to get married at first. The Star Council says we must get married as often as possible and have children. You know why.'

'Why?' I spoke like a small child.

'Because we are lonely. Because there is nothing in the Galaxy except us. You know all that, Hummy.'

The dressing-robot made me a wedding dress – we have robots for everything like that. The dress was white and covered me all over except for my eyes.

My father took my arm.

Buff was waiting with my mother. I saw his eyes through the eye-holes of his wedding suit. They were small mean eyes.

'Hello, Kate,' he said.

My father said, 'Her name is Hummingbird.'

'I know, I know,' Buff said.

'How did you find me?' I asked Buff.

'I had a small camera,' he answered. 'I took a photo of your eyes. Did you know that everybody's eyes are different? Nobody has eyes like yours.'

I turned to my father. 'Listen to him! Can't you see how horrible he is? Please don't make me marry him.'

My father didn't say anything. He couldn't help me.

You *can* say no if a man asks you to marry him on Remembering Night. But you must have a very special reason. A reason that the Star Council will accept. If you are doing work that is important for the Galaxy, the Council will usually accept that as a good reason.

I couldn't think of anything like that. But it was something to hope for . . . if I could escape.

I was afraid. I didn't want to run away and never see my family again.

Some neighbours arrived, and the wedding began immediately.

Buff was waiting with my mother.

Buff stood next to me and held my hand. His hand was large and a little wet. How I hated him!

My father picked up the Book of Remembering. He read, 'In the beginning there were millions of planets in the Galaxy but there was only life on one. That was the planet Earth. People and animals lived together. But people polluted Earth. It became too hot for animals to live. They died. All the animals died. So people left Earth and never returned to that planet. Their hearts were empty when they left Earth, empty today, empty forever . . .'

Buff was still holding my hand.

My father spoke again. 'Buffalo, will you take my daughter Hummingbird to be your wife for one year, in the name of Earth and the animals?'

Buff answered, 'I will.'

My father turned to me. 'Hummingbird, will you take this man Buffalo to be your husband for one year, in the name of Earth and the animals?'

That's when I ran.

I let the wedding dress fall off me. I ran fast. They ran after me but I could run much faster without the wedding dress. I got to our robot spaceship, jumped into it and said, 'Take off.'

'Why are people running towards us?' the spaceship asked.

'Take off now!' I shouted. 'It's life or death!'

The spaceship couldn't argue. It took off.

Just Like Home was green all over – fields of wheat

everywhere. I was out in space looking back at my planet. All around me were stars.

The millions of stars in the Galaxy – that's where I could hide!

2
A spaceship made of plastic

I couldn't believe what I'd done. I'd run away – me!

I'm not very brave and I love my parents very much. I never thought I could ever disobey them.

I was afraid. And I felt sad for my parents. Poor mother and father!

But I had to live my own life. I couldn't get married to a horrible old man like Buffalo!

I knew they would follow me quickly so I told the spaceship to take me to a very quiet part of the Galaxy, a long way from any planets with people on.

The spaceship went.

How can a spaceship travel across the Galaxy in no time at all?

Well, I learnt the answer to that in school. There are a lot of little black holes in space. They are about as big as a potato. A spaceship goes into one black hole and comes out of another black hole on the other side of the Galaxy.

Don't ask me how a big thing like a spaceship can go into a thing as small as a potato. I was probably asleep when the robot teacher told me the answer to that!

Nobody could find me now. I was in the middle of the Galaxy in empty space.

There were stars above my head, stars below my feet, stars on my left hand, stars on my right hand.

Strange. I knew all these stars were a long, long way away but they didn't look far away. They looked very close; I wanted to reach out my hand and touch them.

And the silence. So very, very, very quiet.

The Book of Remembering says how I felt: 'Their hearts were empty.'

My heart was empty. I saw millions of stars but there was no life in the Galaxy except us humans. Well, there are potatoes and wheat and rice but you can't talk to vegetables.

We are alone.

The Book of Remembering says we did it. We polluted Earth and so killed all the animals. We ran away from Earth and we're still running. That was twenty thousand years ago and we still can't forget.

The Book of Remembering gives names for thousands of animals. Fantastic! Could there really be thousands of animals? The idea of animals is so strange. What did they look like? The Book of Remembering has no pictures, but says there are birds that fly, and fish that swim. There are animals with no legs, and animals with lots of legs – ugh! What a horrible idea!

Can *anybody* believe stories like that?

And now I was running away too. Perhaps I was wrong to

run away.

Suddenly the spaceship went 'PING!'

'Yes, what is it?' I asked.

'There is something near us.'

'Oh!' I said. 'I thought we were a long way from anything out here. Take me closer.'

We moved closer, but I couldn't see anything.

Then one star disappeared, then another star, and another. It was too dark to see what the thing was. It was just a big black shape between me and the stars.

It was probably just a big old rock, which had broken off a moon or a planet.

Well, perhaps it contained gold or something. Then I could show the Star Council I was doing important work. Perhaps that would be a good reason not to marry Buff.

I said, 'Find out what it is made of.'

The spaceship shot a laser at the thing and said, 'It is not natural. It may be a spaceship, although it is moving too slowly to arrive at a star. It is made of plastic.'

A spaceship made of plastic? You can't make spaceships out of plastic! And spaceships don't travel slowly.

I was a little afraid, but this was something really important; nobody could make me get married after I had discovered something as strange as this. I was afraid but also excited. Most girls just get married once a year and have another baby. That's enough excitement for them. Not me!

I was going to visit this spaceship and meet . . . the people inside it.

I pulled and pushed and hit the big round door.

'Show me this plastic spaceship,' I said.

My spaceship shone out light. The thing was big, big, BIG. Who would build a spaceship so big? The plastic was full of holes and the spaceship looked old and dead. Would anybody be left alive inside? I didn't think so.

The spaceship was round like a ball. It turned slowly, which made things inside just heavy enough to stay on the ground.

I saw a door on it and said, 'Land there.'

My spaceship landed. I put on a spacesuit, went outside and moved to the big round door. I pulled and pushed and hit it. At last something moved and the door opened.

Inside, there was a tunnel. A long black tunnel. I climbed in and the door closed behind me.

3

Monsters

There was a door at the other end of the tunnel. I went through and . . .

I was dreaming! I saw big things that grew out of the ground. They were much taller than me with long brown arms covered with green leaves.

I was very frightened as I remembered something in the Book of Remembering: 'In those days there were trees . . .'

Trees!

I never thought a living thing could be so big. I covered my eyes with my hands. I was afraid to look . . . but I was afraid *not* to look.

After a time I took my hands away from my eyes. The trees were still there. They weren't moving.

I suddenly understood that the trees *couldn't* move. They were plants, like potatoes or rice. I was safe standing under them.

But I didn't *feel* safe.

The computer inside my spacesuit was checking the air for me. After a few seconds the red lights on my suit turned to green. The air here was safe for humans. So I took off my spacesuit.

Now I could touch and smell things. There was a soft wind. It was cool. I smelt . . . strange new smells. I smelt living things. Was I smelling the trees . . . or something else?

I heard a sound of crying. Then I thought I heard something moving in the trees – just behind one big tree.

Was something hiding behind the tree? I was frightened but I wanted to see, so I walked slowly towards the tree.

There was light in this place but there were shadows in the trees. I looked round the tree . . .

I was frightened almost out of my mind. I fell down and my body started shaking.

A grey thing came out from behind the tree and came towards me. It was big but it wasn't tall because it walked on four feet. It had no hands.

But the thing had teeth. Yes, it had a mouth full of teeth, yellow, shiny teeth. It had yellow eyes and grey hair all over

But the thing had teeth – a mouth full of yellow, shiny teeth.

its body. I could smell it . . .

Its mouth came towards my face. I closed my eyes and waited to die.

There was hot air on my face. I wanted to scream and scream but I was too frightened. I couldn't scream.

My mind exploded. I went crazy. I suddenly hit the grey thing and it fell back against the tree. I hit it again, as hard as I could.

I wanted to destroy the grey thing and I was screaming. Suddenly it was gone.

Then I saw another monster. This one was very small with grey fur all over its body. It was holding on to the tree but I pulled it off. I could destroy this one!

I pulled its short legs hard. The small monster bit me. Its teeth went right into my finger. The pain was terrible.

But my mind was exploding. I wanted to destroy it and I didn't care about the pain. I just wanted to kill it.

Then the big grey monster ran back through the trees, jumped at me and knocked me down. As I fell, I dropped the little monster and it escaped.

My head banged on a rock and everything went black.

4
More monsters

There was a long black nose in front of my face. It was smelling me.

At first I couldn't understand what was happening. Then I remembered. The monster with teeth!

I tried to hit the nose but my arm didn't move. Something was wrong with me. My body felt empty and I was hot inside, like a fire. My body ached and my skin was wet all over.

The big grey monster sat in front of me and it looked at me.

Then I saw the small monster too. It was lying on the ground. It was hurt. It was very small, just a little bigger than my hand. It had a beautiful soft tail and it made a sad sound: 'Eee-eee!'

I felt two different things at the same time. I wanted to destroy it . . . but I also felt sorry for it. It was feeling pain, like me.

I didn't know what to do so I started to cry.

The big monster lay down next to me with its fur against my skin. I hated the feeling of its fur but my body couldn't move.

The fur made my skin dry and I began to feel better. I suddenly felt very tired and I was soon asleep.

I woke up feeling better. I wasn't hot inside and I could move again.

The monsters weren't hurting me. They were helping me.

The big monster sat down with me. I hit it with my hand but I still wasn't strong. I didn't hurt it.

Then the monster opened its mouth and called: 'Hoo-woo!'

Some time passed. Then more monsters came. More and more. Most of the monsters walked on four legs. A very big one licked me with its tongue. It was a hard tongue, not like my soft tongue. But I felt better afterwards. That monster made a noise like this: 'Hee-haw!'

There was a very small monster that could fly. It had wings and a long hard mouth. It made a noise like this: 'Cheep-cheep!'

It cleaned my finger where Eee-Eee had bitten me. Cheep-Cheep's hard little mouth was good at that.

I must tell the truth. I wanted to take a laser gun and kill all those monsters. They weren't hurting me. They were helping me. They were nice.

But something in my mind hated them. I didn't want to have to think about them.

But I didn't have a laser gun so I couldn't destroy them.

One monster brought me water. Another monster gave me some fruit to eat. A few monsters lay against my body and made me warm. They helped me in many ways but there was something sick in my mind. I still hated them.

I will try to explain. For twenty thousand years the Galaxy had belonged to humans. Everything in the Galaxy belonged to us.

When a new baby comes into a family, the first child hates

the baby. The first child wants to be the most important, and to keep everything for itself. It is afraid the baby will take things away from it.

It was like that with me. I wanted to fight these monsters. I didn't want them living with me, in *my* Galaxy.

One day two humans came through the trees. I stood up. I was stronger now. 'Oh, thank Earth-and-animals!' I said and ran towards them.

The humans looked at me with big round eyes. One human was a man with long hair. He said, 'Gug-gug-gug!'

Then he went down on the ground on his hands and knees, like a baby. He ran round me, smelling me.

The woman said, 'Yee-yee-yee!' She jumped up on a branch of a tree.

They were humans but they were just like the monsters. They couldn't talk to me.

I started to feel miserable. The monsters tried to give me food but I didn't care about eating.

The monster that said 'Hee-haw!' carried me on its back and we went to a little river. Hee-Haw dropped me into the water. I didn't care if I was clean or dirty, but Hee-Haw kicked water over me and washed me.

The big grey monster that said 'Hoo-woo!' was worried about me. I didn't eat very much and I didn't wash myself. I just sat.

One day Hoo-Woo came with Hee-Haw. Hee-Haw carried me through the trees and the three of us travelled a long way. Finally we came to a high plastic wall.

Finally we came to a high plastic wall.

Hoo-Woo pushed open a door in the wall and we went through. On the other side the air was hot and wet and the trees were bigger. There were monsters but they were different.

Hee-Haw carried me a long way through this forest. In the end we arrived at another plastic wall where there was another door.

Hoo-Woo opened the door and we entered a long tunnel. At the end of the tunnel was another door. At first Hoo-Woo waited outside this door, looking worried. I looked at the door. What was on the other side? Why was Hoo-Woo so worried? In the end he opened the door.

I saw a small round room just for a second. Then a terrible bright light came out. After that I couldn't see inside any more; it was too bright. I was very frightened. I felt this fear deep inside me.

Hee-Haw's head touched the ground. Hoo-Woo's head touched the ground too. I understood. This was their God! I understood because I felt the same fear as they did.

Hoo-Woo pushed me towards the light.

5
Waiting for fifteen thousand years

'It's too bright in here,' I said. 'I can't see.'

The light suddenly wasn't so bright and I could see again. I was in a round room, which was empty except for a large square computer.

The computer didn't look like the modern computers we have.

'You aren't God!' I said. 'You're just a computer! Just a strange old computer!'

A voice came from it. 'Yes, this is computer. Who are you?'

Oh, the computer still worked! I was surprised as it looked so very old. It didn't speak in a natural way as modern computers do.

'I'm Hummingbird,' I answered.

'You are not a hummingbird. Hummingbirds fly in the forests here, in Star Zoo. You are human. You are not a child of Star Zoo. Computer is happy.'

I listened but I didn't understand. 'Hummingbird' was just my name – and the name of one of the animals in the Book of Remembering. Why was this place called the Star Zoo? What was a 'zoo'? I had so many questions to ask!

'Computer,' I said, 'where do you come from? I never heard of a spaceship as big as this! You speak my language but it sounds different. Why do Hee-Haw and Hoo-Woo think you're God?'

'You aren't God!' I said. 'You're just a computer!
Just a strange old computer!'

'Who is Hee-Haw? Who is Hoo-Woo?' the computer asked.

'The two monsters that brought me here,' I answered.

'Yes. Donkey. Wolf. All animals believe computer is God. Computer makes ultrasonic sound. Ultrasonics make fear.'

'Animals?' I said slowly. Animals were only a story in the Book of Remembering. There were no animals alive today. What was the computer talking about? 'Animals . . . like Eee-Eee and Cheep-Cheep?'

'Eee-Eee is a squirrel,' the computer said. 'Cheep-Cheep is a bird. Animals take care of you.'

I was very afraid. Donkey, wolf, squirrel, and bird were all animals named in the Book of Remembering.

'Where did these animals come from?' I asked.

'Star Zoo came from Earth,' the computer answered. 'Star Zoo left Earth. Earth was hot.'

I suddenly couldn't stand. I fell down and my mind exploded again. This time I wasn't angry. I was sad, empty, afraid, and a little crazy. This was the Book of Remembering come to life!

Earth hot? That was the Burning! We made the Earth too hot and all life except humans died. And we humans did it!

'Not necessary to fall down,' the computer said. 'Computer is not God. Computer wants to talk to humans. Computer is sad that humans have not spoken for fifteen thousand years.'

I stood up slowly. The Book of Remembering was for remembering the animals but they had been dead for twenty thousand years.

But the animals were here! Yes, here in the Star Zoo, after travelling between stars for twenty thousand years!

'Why did you leave Earth? What happened?' I asked.

The computer answered, 'Humans polluted Earth. Earth was hot. Animals died.'

'Yes,' I said. 'I know that.'

The computer continued, 'Humans made zoo in space. No money. Used plastic bottles.'

'What?' I said. I didn't understand.

'Collected old plastic bottles. Made zoo with plastic bottles. Cheap. Made big zoo with many rooms.'

'Why are there different rooms?' I asked.

'Animals and plants live in different ways,' the computer said. 'Hot, cold, wet, dry. Impossible to keep all animals and all plants in one room. Need different things. Difficult work to get everything right. Necessary to have big computer. No money. Got old computer from army.'

'So that's you?' I said. 'You're an old army computer from Earth?'

'Computer works and never stops.'

'I understand!' I said. 'A group of people made this Star Zoo. They knew that Earth was dying. They wanted to save the animals. They sent the Star Zoo away from Earth.'

'Star Zoo went,' the computer said. 'No money. Went slowly.'

'Very slowly,' I agreed. 'But what happened to the humans inside the Star Zoo?'

'Five thousand years humans gave orders. Computer

'Humans polluted Earth. Earth was hot. Animals died,'
said the computer.

worked. Computer mended walls. Computer kept Star Zoo alive and safe. Star Zoo worked well. No problems. Humans stopped giving orders. Not necessary to talk. Humans enjoyed eating, playing, sleeping. Computer can do work. For fifteen thousand years computer has worked, thought, learnt, grown. Now you have come. Computer is happy.'

I was happy too and I wasn't afraid. It was wonderful news. The Galaxy wasn't empty! Animals could live on all the worlds and all humans could be happy again.

Humans were lonely without animals. Humans needed animals.

'The animals must leave the Star Zoo,' I said to the computer. 'We have planets where they can live. Do you agree?'

'Star Zoo is not strong,' the computer said. 'Holes in walls lose air and water. Animals need planets. Can have more animals on planets.'

'Then I must go home,' I said. 'I will come back with spaceships. We will take the animals to different planets. Planets everywhere in the Galaxy.'

'Computer will choose planets for different animals,' it said. 'First plants will grow. Animals will follow.'

'You can tell us what to do,' I said. 'This is wonderful. I want to leave now. Is Hee-Haw waiting?'

'Donkey waits.' The computer made a noise that was like crying. 'Donkey has waited for a few minutes. Computer has waited for fifteen thousand years. You come back. Computer is sad and afraid.'

6
They don't believe me

Where was my spacesuit?

Eee-Eee found it up in a tree where another squirrel was living in it. Eee-Eee told the squirrel to get out of my spacesuit.

I was happy to wear the spacesuit. Hoo-Woo took me to the door where I first came in.

Hoo-Woo made his noise: 'Hoo-woo!' as I opened the door. He was sad that I was going.

I said, 'I'm coming back,' and I went out to my spaceship.

I got in and said, 'Take me home.'

The stars changed suddenly. I saw my world in space, all green and beautiful. A few minutes later the spaceship landed and I was home.

My father ran from the house shouting, 'Hummy!'

I kissed my father.

My mother was angry with me. 'I didn't know if you were dead or alive!' she cried. 'It's been a week!'

A week! It felt like months to me.

'I've got some very exciting news for you,' I said.

'OK,' my mother said. 'Let's sit in the wheat and talk there. Oh yes,' she said to my father, 'why don't you go to the house and bring us something to drink?'

Strange. Robots usually bring the drinks. But I just thought my mother wanted to be specially nice to me.

I told my mother what had happened. When my father

I saw a spaceship land near the house. 'Who's coming?' I asked.

came with drinks, I told my story again.

Telling my story, I looked at the green fields of wheat moving in the wind. The wheat went on for thousands of miles, looking just the same everywhere.

How different it was in the Star Zoo! Every time you turned your head, you saw something new. That had frightened me at first but now I thought the Star Zoo was wonderful.

I explained that feeling to my parents.

'Yes, yes, Hummy,' my mother said, looking quickly at my father.

I saw a spaceship land near the house. 'Who's coming?' I asked.

My mother and father looked at each other. Then I knew.

'It's Buff, isn't it?' I said. 'You called him when you were getting the drinks!' I said to my father. I was really angry. 'How could you? Wait! You don't believe me, do you?'

'Your head is full of dreams, Hummy,' my father said. 'You must be married to Buff, but only for a year. Then you can get married to someone you like.'

I jumped up. 'I hate you! Why did I come back? Why didn't I go straight to the Star Council?'

Buff walked up to us. 'Hello again, Kate,' he said. 'I still remember the first name you told me.'

I had an idea. 'Listen to what happened to me,' I said, and I told my story a third time.

Buff laughed. 'What a story! You can tell me stories like that every night.'

'So you don't believe me?' I smiled.

He just laughed.

'OK, Buff,' I said. 'Come with me. I'll show you the Star Zoo. If it's only a story, I'll marry you. I'll even get married for *five* years if you want. OK?'

'Why not?' Buff said. 'I'll bring a robot to see what's really there. Robots never lie.'

Buff borrowed one of our family robots and we took off. My father watched us go with a worried face.

It was black in the empty space far between stars and we couldn't see anything. Buff was surprised when we landed on the Star Zoo.

We put on spacesuits and went out. Buff looked at the door, very surprised. We went in.

After we went through the second door, Buff stood without moving and he looked at the trees and didn't say anything. The robot closed the door behind us.

Hoo-Woo ran out of the trees to meet me. I was happy to see him and happy to be back in the Star Zoo again. I wasn't afraid at all.

I looked round at Buff and my heart stopped. Buff's face was full of hate and he was holding a laser gun. The gun was pointing at Hoo-Woo.

Buff's face was full of hate and he was holding a laser gun.

7
The answer is robots

I pushed Buff as he tried to shoot Hoo-Woo. The laser gun burnt a hole in the plastic wall, but it didn't hit Hoo-Woo.

Buff was screaming and the whites of his eyes were showing. He fell on the ground and water ran out of his mouth. He was crazy. I remembered the way I had gone crazy when I first came into the Star Zoo. It was seeing the animals. It was the Book of Remembering coming to life. It made people go crazy.

I hid Buff's laser gun and used some long plants to tie him up. Hee-Haw sat on him while I did it. A bell was ringing and all the animals started looking for something. What were they looking for?

A bird found it. It was the hole where the laser had burnt through the wall. The Star Zoo was losing air. I could hear the air escaping.

It was the computer's job to check for damage like that. Then it rang the bell. But how could the animals mend the hole?

Eee-Eee went to a pipe on the wall and waited. Warm wet plastic came out of the end of the pipe. The squirrel held little bits of the plastic and ran quickly up the wall. She put the soft plastic over the hole and ran down to get more plastic from the pipe.

In one minute the hole was covered. Eee-Eee went on working until the bell stopped ringing.

The computer and the animals worked together to mend the Star Zoo. After fifteen thousand years they were very good at it!

Buff had crazy eyes. The animals didn't want to go near him so I took care of him. I hoped he would get better soon.

But he didn't get better. Three days later he still wanted to kill and destroy every animal that he saw. He thought I was an animal too.

He never spoke. Perhaps he had forgotten how to speak. He wouldn't touch food or water.

I didn't know what to do. In the end I went to see the computer with Hee-Haw and the robot.

There was the same terrible light and the fear. But I knew it was ultrasonics that made me afraid. The robot didn't have any feelings, of course. The robot and I went into the computer room but Hee-Haw stayed outside.

The ultrasonics stopped and the light went soft.

'Hummingbird,' the computer said. 'You have come back. Computer is happy. Who is the other human?'

'This isn't a human,' I explained. 'This is just a family robot.'

'Not human? Looks very human.'

'I know,' I said. 'But that's not important. Everything's gone crazy!'

'What is the problem?' the computer asked.

I told the computer about visiting my parents and that they didn't believe me. I explained about Buff and said, 'But he's gone crazy. I know I went crazy at first but I got better.

'This isn't a human,' I explained. 'This is just a family robot.'

Buff isn't getting better.'

'Why?' the computer said. 'You are human. Buff is human. What is different?'

'I don't know,' I answered. 'I'm younger than Buff. Perhaps people's minds get hard like rock as they get older. They can't change how they think.'

'When will Buff get better?' the computer asked.

'Never . . . I think,' I said. 'Buff's too old.'

There was silence. After a long time the computer said slowly, 'Computer is old.'

'Oh, that's different,' I said. 'I think you are growing very, very slowly. I think you're still young, like me. You're still growing and changing. Not like Buff.'

Another silence. Then, 'Hummingbird is friend.'

I felt wonderful. The computer was twenty thousand years old and it wanted to be friends with me!

'Yes, I'm your friend, computer,' I said. 'I'll be your friend all my life, but my life isn't long like yours. Perhaps my children and grandchildren can be your friends too.'

'Computer is happy.'

'Oh, computer, everything's finished!' I said. 'I thought Buff could learn to accept the animals like me, but he can't. He can't change how he thinks. And I think most people in the Galaxy are like him. They can't change. If they find the Star Zoo, they'll destroy all the animals. So it's impossible! We can't put the animals on different planets. The animals will have to stay in the Star Zoo. One day the Star Zoo will die. After that there will be no life in the Galaxy except humans. Forever.'

The computer said, 'Computer will find answer to problem. Wait.'

I waited. And waited. I couldn't understand it. Computers think so fast! Why wasn't the computer telling me the answer?

At last it spoke. 'Computer has answer to problem. The answer is robots. Your robot looks very human. You will make a robot like an animal. Humans will know it is a robot, not an animal. Humans will not go crazy. Humans will learn about animals. After some time humans will meet animals. Humans will not go crazy.'

'I think I understand,' I said. 'People have to spend a long time with robot animals first. When they are not afraid, they can meet the real animals and accept them. Yes, it's a wonderful idea, computer! I could kiss you!'

'Nobody has kissed computer. Computer is interested.'

So I kissed the computer and I think it kissed me.

8
An animal is made

A robot can do many different things from taking care of a baby to building a spaceship. It can do anything except think. The Star Zoo computer was the only one that could think.

Well, our family robot could build a robot animal, easily. That was no problem.

First we had to choose what animal to make, so we went round the Star Zoo to look at all the animals. Hee-Haw carried me and Hoo-Woo came with us. The robot followed.

I don't know how many rooms the Star Zoo had; I couldn't count them all. Some rooms were filled with water where there were big fish and small fish. There were horrible monsters walking under the water and I felt a little afraid again.

Some rooms were covered in snow and all the animals there had white fur. There were dry rooms, hot wet rooms, forest rooms . . . And animals and birds and trees and flowers!

There were more living things than I had ever dreamt of!

I sat on Hee-Haw's back as the donkey walked on. We went through a door into a room full of strange life, then we went through another door and into another room. It was like a dream. In a dream, things change suddenly, without reason. It was like that.

We went back to the computer. I didn't know which

*Some rooms were filled with water where there were big fish
and small fish.*

animal to choose and neither did the robot. Hee-Haw and Hoo-Woo didn't understand the problem; they weren't intelligent in the human way.

So I asked the computer.

'Watch humans,' the computer said. 'Humans enjoy playing with animals. Find an animal which enjoys playing with humans.'

So we went to see the humans.

The humans in the Star Zoo couldn't speak. I sat down and watched them while the humans played up in the trees, swam in the pool and played games in the grass. They played all the time.

Most other animals didn't play with the humans. But finally I saw one animal come through the grass to play. It liked playing with humans!

The humans played with the animal for an hour. The animal and the humans enjoyed playing together.

'That's the animal you must make,' I told the robot.

The robot watched the animal and touched it and measured everything. In the end it was ready to build a robot just like that animal.

'What do you need to build it?' I asked.

'Plastic,' the robot answered. 'I will use real fur on the outside. But I need some metal. Where can I find metal?'

There was only one thing in the Star Zoo made of metal – the computer!

The computer told the robot to take off two small pieces of metal from its back.

The robot worked fast. Sometimes it needed a special tool. Then it opened its stomach because the tools were kept inside the body there.

First, the robot made a plastic body which it covered with soft plastic, like a skin. Then it used fur to cover the skin.

I left before the robot finished because I was worried about Buff. I didn't want him to die.

Buff still wouldn't eat or drink. But the worst thing was, he was still crazy. His mind wasn't getting better . . .

If Buff stays in the Star Zoo, I thought, he'll die.

I talked to him but he didn't answer. I knew he wanted to kill me. He wanted to kill all living things.

The robot finished its work and showed me a little animal. It looked, and sounded, and played like the real animal. I took it to the computer.

'Yes, it looks just like the animal,' the computer said. 'It's very small – a baby animal.' The computer told me its name. It checked the animal, then said to the robot, 'Make it warm.'

The little animal was cold.

So the robot made the baby animal warm, like the real animal. We were ready.

The robot put Buff to sleep, then put the spacesuit on him and carried him to the spaceship.

I was leaving the Star Zoo for the second time. Would our plan succeed, I wondered? Before I went through the door, I looked back – at all the life that existed only here in the Star Zoo, and in no other place in all the Galaxy!

First the robot made a plastic body which it covered with
soft plastic, like a skin.

9

An animal is destroyed

Buff was asleep. I told the spaceship to take us to New Earth, the planet of the Star Council. I wasn't going back to my parents. I wanted to go to the top people.

A few minutes later the spaceship was falling towards a planet covered with tall buildings. Many of the buildings touched the clouds. I'd never been to New Earth before. I was just a young girl from a small planet and I felt very unimportant here.

We landed. I could see a lot of people walking quickly. They didn't stand and talk. They were too busy. Who was going to stop and talk to a young girl like me?

Everybody was wearing very expensive, fashionable clothes too! I felt stupid with just my old clothes with my name 'Hummingbird' on. I said to the robot, 'Make a special dress for me. I want to look more important.'

A minute later I had the dress. It didn't look very good. It was grey and just like an old bag.

I put on the dress and it suddenly came to life. It moved over me, full of changing colours. When I looked in a mirror, I couldn't believe it. I looked fantastic!

When I got out of the spaceship, I wasn't afraid of anybody.

At first I thought the Star Council buildings were the high ones, up in the clouds. They weren't. I had to go below ground to an office where I spoke to a policeman. He didn't

A few minutes later the spaceship was falling towards a planet covered with tall buildings.

believe my story about the Star Zoo . . . until the robot told him it was all true. Robots can't lie.

The policeman looked at me for a long time. In the end he called a Star Council official.

He and the policeman took me to a lift and we went down many floors. Then they put me in a room and asked me questions. They wanted to see the robot animal but I said no. I said only the Star Council could see the robot animal.

Three hours later they were still asking me questions and I couldn't keep my eyes open. I was so tired. My dress had lost its colours. It was just grey again. I didn't feel important. I felt like a child.

But I didn't show them the robot animal.

The official said, 'I don't believe you. There are no animals in the Galaxy now. Perhaps there never were any animals. They're only stories in the Book of Remembering.'

'Well, why are you asking me so many questions?' I said.

'Because your robot tells the same story. Because you have a crazy man in your spaceship – he's in hospital now.'

Suddenly the official got up and took me to the lift. We went down, down, down, very fast.

We came out into a room in the shape of a star. I felt frightened because I knew this was the Star Room where the Star Council met.

The Council men and women came in and took their places at the Star Table. The official told them my story, which my robot repeated.

Everybody looked at me, waiting for me to show them the

robot animal.

The President of the Star Council said, 'Where is this animal?'

'It's not an animal,' I said. 'It's a robot. But it looks just the same as a real animal.'

'Where is it?'

I touched the robot's stomach. 'In there,' I answered.

'Bring it out. We want to see it,' the President said.

'Yes, sir,' I said. I looked round at all the Councillors. I was afraid to speak to these important people but I had to tell them about the danger. 'When Buff saw an animal, he went crazy. I went crazy at first, too.'

'We heard your story.'

'Please listen,' I said. 'This is a robot. Please remember it's not a real animal. I don't want anybody here to go crazy.'

'Don't try to frighten us, girl. Bring out the animal.'

I told the robot to open its stomach, and it opened. The little robot animal jumped on to the Star Table.

It looked so alive! It opened its mouth and made the special noise of that animal. It had small sharp white teeth.

The mouth of every Councillor fell open at the same moment.

There was a sudden bright light. The little animal exploded. It was gone. There was nothing left except a little wet plastic on the Star Table and a smell of burning hair.

The Star Council official had destroyed it with his laser gun.

The Councillors were getting up and shouting. Their faces

There was a sudden bright light. The little animal exploded. It was gone.

were full of hate. They had the same crazy eyes as Buff. Perhaps not as bad as Buff, because the animal had only been there for a second or two and I had told them it was a robot. But, like Buff, they wanted to kill and destroy.

Things got worse and worse. They started breaking chairs. Some of them used broken chairs to hit people. They were going crazy, just like Buff.

The plan had failed. The Star Council had gone crazy. I was very frightened. What had I done?

10
Two of everything

It was a strange prison with no doors and no police to watch me. Well, I didn't know the special number for making the lifts work, so I couldn't escape by the lifts. There were stairs but it was ten kilometres straight up to get to the surface.

I couldn't get out.

I found food and water. Nobody came to see me for three days.

Finally a soldier arrived and took me back to the Star Room.

An old man with a very straight back sat at the Star Table. He was alone and looked tired. 'Hummingbird,' he said and then stopped.

'Who are you, please?' I asked. I hadn't seen him before.

'I'm the new President,' he said, but he didn't sound happy

about it.

'So the President and the Councillors are still . . .'

'Still crazy – yes,' the old man said. 'I think many of them will get better. They saw the animal only for a very short time.'

'It wasn't a real animal,' I said quickly.

'That didn't make any difference. You asked me who I am. I'm just one of the Star Councillors, but I wasn't in the Star Room when you showed them the animal. I was lucky. Now listen, Hummingbird. There is something I must tell you. Something difficult.'

'Is it about my family?' I asked, feeling afraid.

'No, Hummingbird. You are the only person in the Galaxy who knows where the Star Zoo is. If other people know about the Star Zoo, there will be killing. People will be killed. The Star Zoo will be destroyed. It is very important to keep the Star Zoo alive and so it is necessary to keep it secret. I'm sorry, Hummingbird. You must stay here, ten kilometres down, all your life. I know you're a young girl and I'm sorry.'

'All my life?' I said. I couldn't believe it.

'Yes,' the old man said. 'This is the planet of the Star Council so there is always work here you can do. I'm sorry.'

'What kind of work?' I asked.

'Well, everything is going crazy now. For example, we have some little children down here that nobody is taking care of. A robot is doing the job now – but little children need real humans. Would you like to try taking care of them?'

'OK,' I said. It was something to do.

I went to see the children, who were playing quietly with a robot. I laughed, because the robot was our family robot. I thought this robot and I would do something wonderful. But we could only take care of little children!

I sat on the floor and played with the children. They were all less than four years old.

They needed somebody. A few of the children were crying. They needed loving. Robots can sing and play games, but they can't love.

Only the Star Zoo computer can love.

Soon one little boy was sitting on my stomach and another boy was running round and round me. A little girl was pulling my hair and another girl was biting my finger. There was a lot of noise.

These children were more trouble than any animal in the Star Zoo!

'These girls and boys aren't going to be afraid of animals,' I said to the robot. 'I can show *them* a robot animal and they won't go crazy. I just wish I had one.'

'You have,' the robot answered. 'Shall I take out the other one?'

'What!' I shouted. The little boy fell off my stomach and began screaming. I picked him up and kissed him until the screaming changed to crying. I said, 'Another robot animal?'

'Yes,' the robot said, touching its stomach.

Of course the robot had another! Robots always make two of everything. You don't have to tell them. They do it automatically.

These children were more trouble than any animal in the Star Zoo!

The robot opened its stomach and the second robot animal jumped out. It was just like the first one.

The little boy stopped crying. He looked at the robot animal with big, round eyes. All the other children were looking, too.

The animal began to play. It tried to bite its tail and fell over its own feet. It was a funny, sweet animal. After one minute the children were round it in a circle, laughing and playing with it, just like the humans in the Star Zoo.

I watched them. This was very important. These children hadn't learnt to be afraid of animals because they had never heard of Earth, the Burning, or the Book of Remembering.

I watched and thought. I spoke softly to my robot: 'If these children go on playing with this robot animal, they will never become afraid of animals. They won't go crazy.' I thought some more, and said, 'But if their parents see the animal, the parents *will* go crazy.'

I thought carefully. Yes, there must be a special room in every house. A room which parents couldn't go in. A room for children only. Then children could play with robot animals in that room.

'That's it!' I said. 'The children will still be happy to be with animals when *they* are parents. It might take twenty, thirty, forty years, but then —'

I heard the sound of somebody coming. I shouted to the robot, 'Hide that animal, quick!'

The robot opened its stomach and the animal went inside.

All the children began crying. They wanted to have their

'It's called a kitten.'

wonderful animal back again!

It was the President. He looked round at all the crying children. 'Did I do this?' he asked.

'No,' I answered. 'Please stay. I have fantastic news for you. Listen to what just happened.'

The old man listened. First he was angry, then he was surprised but in the end he became very excited.

'Hummingbird,' the President said, 'I must not see that robot animal. I don't want to go crazy. Your idea is . . . interesting. I think it will work. We must be very careful. We

can begin with just one family and can learn from our mistakes. I think we can let you go free, Hummingbird.'

'You can see the animal again soon,' I promised the children, and kissed the ones that were still crying.

'So the little children really liked this animal!' the President said. 'What kind of animal was it? Does the Book of Remembering talk about it?'

'The Book of Remembering talks about cats,' I answered. 'This is a baby cat. I can't remember what the computer called it. Oh yes I do – it's called a kitten.'

GLOSSARY

buffalo   a wild animal, like a large cow

caterpillar   a very small, long, thin animal with many legs, which eats leaves

council   a group of people chosen to work together and make rules or laws

donkey   an animal like a small horse, with long ears

Earth   the planet where we live

exist   to be real or alive

fur   the thick soft hair that covers the bodies of many animals

galaxy   a very big group of millions of stars

God   the being that some people believe made the world

horrible   very bad, making you afraid or unhappy

human *(n)*   a person (man, woman, or child)

hummingbird   a very small, brightly coloured bird that makes a humming sound (a low, continuous sound) with its wings

kiss *(v)*   to touch someone with your lips to show friendly or loving feelings

kitten   a young cat

laser   a thin line of very strong light, made by a special machine and used for burning holes in things

laser gun   a gun which uses burning laser light to kill or hurt people

lick *(v)*   to pass the tongue over something

metal   most machines are made of some kind of metal

mind *(n)*   the part of a person that thinks, feels, and remembers

monster   a large, strange animal or person that is very frightening

planet a large round thing in space (e.g. the Earth), which goes round the sun or any other star

plastic light, strong stuff made in factories; bottles are often made of plastic

pollute to make a place (air, water, or land) very dirty and dangerous to live in

robot a machine that looks like and can do the jobs of many humans

space the emptiness between all stars, planets, and galaxies

spaceship a machine for travelling through space between stars and planets

spacesuit special clothes over all the head and body for travelling in space

squirrel a small grey or red animal with a big soft tail, which lives in trees

tool a thing you hold in your hand and use to work on something

tunnel a long narrow hole which goes from one place to another

ultrasonic a very high sound which humans cannot hear

wheat a plant which is used to make bread

wolf a wild animal like a big dog

zoo a place where many different kinds of wild animals are kept for people to look at

The Star Zoo

ACTIVITIES

Before Reading

1 **Read the story introduction on the first page of the book, and the back cover. What do you know now about the story? Choose T (true) or F (false) for each sentence.**

1 This story happens a long way in the future. T/F
2 Hummy lives on a planet called Earth. T/F
3 She is married. T/F
4 She lives in a place without animals or birds. T/F
5 She thinks the Book of Remembering is all true. T/F

2 **Match these explanations with these words from the story.**

a person, not an animal	believe
the time that has not happened yet	the Earth
the emptiness between the stars	the future
the planet that we live on	a galaxy
to think that something is true	a human
a very big group of millions of stars	space

3 **What is the Star Zoo in this story? Can you guess? Choose one of these ideas.**

1 A place where animals from other galaxies are kept.
2 A place on Earth where people go to look at stars.
3 A zoo somewhere in space with animals from Earth in it.
4 A zoo with some very famous animals in it.

While Reading

Read Chapters 1 and 2. Choose the best question-word for these questions, and then answer them.

What / Where / Why

1 . . . did humans leave the planet Earth?

2 . . . happened to all the animals on Earth?

3 . . . were people lonely and sad?

4 . . . did Buff first see Hummy?

5 . . . couldn't Hummy refuse to marry Buff?

6 . . . did Hummy do before the end of her wedding?

7 . . . did Hummy tell her robot spaceship to take her?

8 . . . did Hummy hope to find gold in the strange spaceship?

9 . . . was the strange spaceship made of?

Read Chapters 3 and 4. What happened to Hummy in the Star Zoo? Make some sentences from this table.

	carried	Hummy's bitten finger.
The wolf	brought	Hummy in the river.
The squirrel	bit	Hummy's skin with its fur.
The donkey	cleaned	Hummy with its tongue.
The bird	dried	Hummy food and water.
Some of them	licked	Hummy on its back.
	washed	Hummy's finger.

Before you read Chapter 5, can you guess what happens next? Choose answers to these questions.

1 Who or what does Hummy find in the round room?
 a person / a monster / a computer / a video / a God
2 How does Hummy feel in the room? Choose five of these.
 surprised / bored / afraid / angry / sad / happy / excited
3 When does Hummy leave the Star Zoo?
 immediately / after two weeks / after a year / never

Read Chapters 5 and 6. Here are some untrue sentences. Rewrite them with the correct information.

1 The Star Zoo had always existed in space.
2 The zoo was made of glass and metal, and had one room.
3 The humans had stopped talking because they were crazy.
4 The plan was to take animals to one planet in the Galaxy.
5 Buff went back with Hummy to the Star Zoo because he was excited about the animals.

Before you read Chapter 7, what do you think will happen next? Choose Y (yes) or N (no) for each of these ideas.

1 Buff shoots at the wolf with his laser gun, misses him, but burns a hole in the spaceship's plastic wall. Y/N
2 Buff shoots the wolf, and the wolf dies. Y/N
3 The wolf bites Buff on the leg, and Buff dies later. Y/N
4 Hummy takes the gun from Buff and shoots him. Y/N
5 Buff goes crazy and Hummy has to tie him up. Y/N

Read Chapters 7 and 8, then complete these sentences.

1 The computer rang a bell, and _____.
2 Hummy took care of Buff, but _____.
3 Hummy realized that they could never take any animals out of the Star Zoo because _____.
4 The computer thought that they could use a robot animal to _____.
5 The computer told Hummy to choose an animal that _____.
6 The robot made the animal, using _____.

Before you read Chapter 9 (*An animal is destroyed*), try to guess the answers to these questions.

1 What kind of animal has Hummy's family robot made?
2 Who will destroy it, and why?

Read Chapters 9 and 10, and then answer these questions.

Why

1 ... did Hummy want a new dress for New Earth?
2 ... did the official agree to take Hummy to the Star Council?
3 ... did the Councillors go crazy?
4 ... wasn't Hummy allowed to leave?
5 ... did the robot have another animal in its stomach?
6 ... weren't the children afraid of the robot animal?
7 ... did the President let Hummy go free?

After Reading

1 **Perhaps this is what some of the characters in the story (human and non-human) were thinking. Which characters are they, and what is happening in the story at this moment? Put the thoughts in the right order for the story.**

1 'Well, this part of her story is true, and it seems to be a very old spaceship. The robot's opening the inside door now, so in a second I'll see . . . No . . . No! . . . Aaargh! What's that? It's coming towards me!'

2 'The door has opened. Something in the tunnel. The inside door has opened . . . and shut. No danger. No air escaping. But who is it? What is it? Wait and see. What are a few more days after fifteen thousand years?'

3 'Yes, I think her plan has a good chance of working. But we must choose the family carefully. I wish I could see the animal myself – No, no, I mustn't. It's too dangerous . . .'

4 'I'll call him on the videophone while I'm getting the drinks. I don't want to do it, but I have to. We've all got to follow the Star Council's orders. She'll have to learn that, poor girl . . .'

5 'Four legs and a tail. Big green eyes and small ears. Covered in black fur. I have the necessary tools and I can use plastic for most of it. But I'll need metal as well . . .'

2 Perhaps Hummy sent news to her parents by e-mail, and they sent e-mails back. Put the e-mails in the right order, and write in the senders' names. Number 3 is the first e-mail.

1 _____ 'Of course it's real! Why don't you believe me?'

2 _____ 'Important work for the galaxy? What *are* you talking about, Hummy?'

3 _____ 'Hi! Just wanted to tell you that I'm fine, and that I'm on New Earth, in the Star Council building.'

4 _____ 'Why? What's happened? Has he had an accident?'

5 _____ 'It's about the animals, but it'll take too long to explain now. I'll tell you when I see you.'

6 _____ 'But, Hummy, you'll have to marry someone.'

7 _____ 'He's in hospital.'

8 _____ 'We thought it was just a story you were telling, Hummy – because you didn't want to marry Buffalo.'

9 _____ 'Don't know. I'm going back to the Star Zoo tomorrow, to begin my work. So bye for now!'

10 _____ 'The Star Zoo? You mean it's real? It exists?'

11 _____ 'No, I won't. I'm doing important work for the galaxy so I don't have to get married if I don't want to.'

12 _____ 'What are you doing on New Earth, Hummy? And where's Buffalo?'

13 _____ 'No, but he's gone crazy, I'm afraid. It happened when he saw the animals in the Star Zoo.'

14 _____ 'When will that be? When are you coming home?'

15 _____ 'Well, it's *not* a story – and I'm not going to marry Buff now he's crazy.'

3 There are 22 words (4 letters or longer) from the story in this word search. They go from left to right, and from top to bottom. Find them and draw lines through them.

I	D	O	N	K	E	Y	T	H	U	M	A	N	B
E	S	Q	U	I	R	R	E	L	C	E	N	A	M
C	P	E	T	T	O	O	L	O	P	T	I	O	H
O	A	C	O	T	B	B	T	F	L	A	M	O	R
M	C	O	T	E	I	O	A	G	A	L	A	X	Y
P	E	U	R	N	R	T	N	I	N	W	L	W	L
U	S	N	E	M	D	A	L	S	E	H	T	O	A
T	H	C	E	P	O	L	L	U	T	E	O	L	S
E	I	I	E	A	R	T	H	L	I	A	V	F	E
R	P	L	A	S	T	I	C	E	S	T	A	R	R

4 Use 10 words from the word search to complete this passage about Hummy's world. (You will need to make some of the words plural.)

Hummy lives on a _____ where there are no _____, just fields of _____ that go on for miles and miles. All the work in the house is done by family _____, which look and talk like _____. Travelling through space is easy, and people can go in their _____ from one side of the _____ to the other. Nobody has ever seen an _____ or a _____ because they all died on _____ 20,000 years before.

Would *you* like to live in a future world like this? Why, or why not?

5 Look at the word search again, and write down all the letters that don't have a line through them. Begin with the first line and go across each line to the end. You should have 30 letters, which will make a sentence of 8 words.

1 What is the sentence, and where was it written?

2 What was the sentence about?

3 Does this sentence have a message for us in the real world today? If so, what do you think the message is?

6 Do you agree (A) or disagree (D) with these ideas? Explain why.

1 We should not allow any animals to die out and disappear.

2 Animal lives are just as important as human lives.

3 There is a real danger that humans will pollute this planet very badly, and many, if not all, animals will die.

4 There will always be millions of different kinds of animals and plants on Earth. It doesn't matter if a few die.

5 As the planet gets hotter or colder over the centuries, animals and plants learn to change.

6 Some of the animals that we know today will disappear. In 20,000 years' time there will be new and very different animals on Earth.

7 Imagine that Earth is now too hot to live on. You are leaving for a planet in a galaxy far away, and you can take ten animals (a male and a female of each) with you. Which animals will you choose, and why?

ABOUT THE AUTHOR

Harry Gilbert was born in Canada in 1946 and came to England when he was a baby. After university, he travelled in many parts of the world, doing various jobs, including teaching English as a Foreign Language. He is married, with one daughter, and now lives and teaches in London. As well as *The Star Zoo*, he has written *The Year of Sharing* (at Stage 2) for the Oxford Bookworms Library, and he has also written several books for English children.

Harry Gilbert fell in love with science fiction when he was eleven years old, and spent the next five years reading every science-fiction story he could find, and also writing his own stories. He says that getting ideas for stories is hard work. The ideas for *The Year of Sharing* and *The Star Zoo* came to him while he was watching students during their examinations.

OXFORD BOOKWORMS LIBRARY

Classics • Crime & Mystery • Factfiles • Fantasy & Horror
Human Interest • Playscripts • Thriller & Adventure
True Stories • World Stories

The OXFORD BOOKWORMS LIBRARY provides enjoyable reading in English, with a wide range of classic and modern fiction, non-fiction, and plays. It includes original and adapted texts in seven carefully graded language stages, which take learners from beginner to advanced level. An overview is given on the next pages.

All Stage 1 titles are available as audio recordings, as well as over eighty other titles from Starter to Stage 6. All Starters and many titles at Stages 1 to 4 are specially recommended for younger learners. Every Bookworm is illustrated, and Starters and Factfiles have full-colour illustrations.

The OXFORD BOOKWORMS LIBRARY also offers extensive support. Each book contains an introduction to the story, notes about the author, a glossary, and activities. Additional resources include tests and worksheets, and answers for these and for the activities in the books. There is advice on running a class library, using audio recordings, and the many ways of using Oxford Bookworms in reading programmes. Resource materials are available on the website <www.oup.com/bookworms>.

The *Oxford Bookworms Collection* is a series for advanced learners. It consists of volumes of short stories by well-known authors, both classic and modern. Texts are not abridged or adapted in any way, but carefully selected to be accessible to the advanced student.

You can find details and a full list of titles in the *Oxford Bookworms Library Catalogue* and *Oxford English Language Teaching Catalogues*, and on the website <www.oup.com/bookworms>.

THE OXFORD BOOKWORMS LIBRARY
GRADING AND SAMPLE EXTRACTS

STARTER • 250 HEADWORDS

present simple – present continuous – imperative –
can/cannot, must – going to (future) – simple gerunds …

Her phone is ringing – but where is it?

Sally gets out of bed and looks in her bag. No phone. She looks under the bed. No phone. Then she looks behind the door. There is her phone. Sally picks up her phone and answers it. ***Sally's Phone***

STAGE 1 • 400 HEADWORDS

… past simple – coordination with *and, but, or* –
subordination with *before, after, when, because, so* …

I knew him in Persia. He was a famous builder and I worked with him there. For a time I was his friend, but not for long. When he came to Paris, I came after him – I wanted to watch him. He was a very clever, very dangerous man. ***The Phantom of the Opera***

STAGE 2 • 700 HEADWORDS

… present perfect – *will* (future) – *(don't) have to, must not, could* –
comparison of adjectives – simple *if* clauses – past continuous –
tag questions – *ask/tell* + infinitive …

While I was writing these words in my diary, I decided what to do. I must try to escape. I shall try to get down the wall outside. The window is high above the ground, but I have to try. I shall take some of the gold with me – if I escape, perhaps it will be helpful later. ***Dracula***

... should, may – present perfect continuous – *used to* – past perfect –
causative – relative clauses – indirect statements ...

Of course, it was most important that no one should see
Colin, Mary, or Dickon entering the secret garden. So Colin
gave orders to the gardeners that they must all keep away
from that part of the garden in future. *The Secret Garden*

STAGE 4 • 1400 HEADWORDS

... past perfect continuous – passive (simple forms) –
would conditional clauses – indirect questions –
relatives with *where/when* – gerunds after prepositions/phrases ...

I was glad. Now Hyde could not show his face to the world
again. If he did, every honest man in London would be proud
to report him to the police. *Dr Jekyll and Mr Hyde*

STAGE 5 • 1800 HEADWORDS

... future continuous – future perfect –
passive (modals, continuous forms) –
would have conditional clauses – modals + perfect infinitive ...

If he had spoken Estella's name, I would have hit him. I was so
angry with him, and so depressed about my future, that I could
not eat the breakfast. Instead I went straight to the old house.
Great Expectations

STAGE 6 • 2500 HEADWORDS

... passive (infinitives, gerunds) – advanced modal meanings –
clauses of concession, condition

When I stepped up to the piano, I was confident. It was as if I
knew that the prodigy side of me really did exist. And when I
started to play, I was so caught up in how lovely I looked that
I didn't worry how I would sound. *The Joy Luck Club*

Frankenstein

MARY SHELLEY

Retold by Patrick Nobes

Victor Frankenstein thinks he has found the secret of life. He takes parts from dead people and builds a new 'man'. But this monster is so big and frightening that everyone runs away from him – even Frankenstein himself!

The monster is like an enormous baby who needs love. But nobody gives him love, and soon he learns to hate. And, because he is so strong, the next thing he learns is how to kill …

Wyatt's Hurricane

DESMOND BAGLEY

Retold by Jennifer Bassett

Hurricane Mabel is far out in the Atlantic Ocean and moving slowly northwards. Perhaps it will never come near land at all. But if it hits the island of San Fernandez, many thousands of people will die. There could be winds of more than 250 kilometres an hour. There could be a huge tidal wave from the sea, which will drown the capital city of St Pierre. Mabel will destroy houses, farms, roads, bridges …

Only one man, David Wyatt, believes that Mabel will hit San Fernandez, but nobody will listen to him …